NOW WHAT?

GETTING THE HANG OF CHRISTIANITY

Loretta Andrews

THOMAS NELSON PUBLISHERS
NASHVILLE
A Division of Thomas Nelson. Inc.

www.ThomasNelson.com
www.Xt4J.com

First published 2001 by Word Publishing, 9 Holdom Avenue, Bletchley, Milton Keynes, Bucks, MK1 1QR, UK

Scripture quotations are taken from the Holy Bible New Century Version Copyright © 1987, 1988, 1991 by Word Publishing, a division of Thomas Nelson, Inc.

Library of Congress Cataloging-in-Publication Data

Andrews, L. (Loretta)
   Now what? : getting the hang of Christianity / L. Andrews.
      p. cm.
   ISBN 0-7852-6404-3
   1. Teenagers—Religious life. 2. Teenagers—Conduct of life. I. Title.
BV4531.3 .A545 2002
248.8'3—dc21   2002007197

Printed in the United States of America
1 2 3 4 5 — 06 05 04 03 02

THANKS

Special thanks to everyone who has helped to make this book happen: Malcom Down and everyone at Word Publishing, John and Sue Ritter, Mark and Gareth, and everyone at Alliance.

Thanks and big hugs to all my guinea pigs who contributed and let me test it out on them—the other Shine girlies Han, Nic, and Tash; Claire Hendy from Leon School, Lucy Quist and Abbey Cunningham who are members of a local church youth group, and David Fenton.

This book is dedicated to all the pupils Shine has met in the Milton Keynes Secondary Schools.

Contents

I did not grow up in a Christian family, but I became a Christian at the age of fourteen. I had never really believed that we just live, die, and that's it! So, the first time I heard about how much God loves me, what Jesus has done for me, and how I could get in on life to the full, I just knew it was the Truth and knew I didn't want to miss out on it. I thought to myself: *How do I know if this works?*

Anything else seems like 2nd best in comparison.

Well, how do you know anything works?—by trying it! So I did, and in the last ten years God has proven Himself to be real to me time and time again. But what a journey it has been. Don't let anyone tell you it's easy being a Christian (in fact, Jesus said just the opposite), but it is the most fulfilling life there is and, frankly, anything else seems like second best in comparison.

The morning after I became a Christian, I remember having a bit of a panic attack and thinking *Oh no, what if I've done the wrong thing by becoming a Christian—is this what I really want?* All sorts of other doubts and fears came into my head. I knew I'd made a huge, significant decision that would affect my whole life and, to be honest, it was pretty scary. But then I thought to myself: *If this stuff is really true then of course I want it,* so I decided then and there to stick to it.

However, I still felt more than a little overwhelmed and lost, and wondered how to start living this new life on a daily basis. I had all sorts of questions that I was too scared to ask and felt guilty for having doubts, too. I have since found that what I was feeling was perfectly understandable and normal for a "baby Christian" (as I was)—but I didn't realize it at the time. Because of this experience, it has always been my ambition to write a book like this and dedicate it to all people out there who have either just made that decision or are thinking it through and are feeling exactly the way I did. Hey, you're normal! It's okay to have doubts, and it's okay to have questions—there are answers—it's all part of stepping into this new and amazing adventure called "life with God." So I hope this helps you.

INTRoDUCTiON

As part of one of our lessons in the Milton Keynes schools (that's where we do a lot of our work), we conducted a little survey to find out what things are important in the lives of teens. We asked three questions. How about you answer them, too?

1. What is your most precious possession?
2. What is your happiest moment?
3. What is your biggest ambition?

Another recent survey showed that most people believe that in order to be happy and fulfilled they need to have one or more of the following: money, freedom, relationships, career, popularity, and looks. Amazingly, in each class every answer someone gave fit into one or more of these six categories. I'm sure you will find the same with your answers. For example, if your most precious possession is your mom, that comes under relationships; or if your happiest moment was when you did a bungee jump, that would come under freedom; and if your biggest ambition is to play professional soccer, that could come under money, career, and popularity.

Money, Freedom, Relationships, Career, Popularity & Looks

However, if all our happiness and fulfillment is based *only* on these six categories, we are faced with a problem. Take a closer look at the six categories. Okay, so there is nothing wrong with wanting any of these things. Actually, most of us would admit to being happier with some or all of them— *but,* all of these things can come to an end, breakdown, run out, or fail you. So what then? What becomes of our happiness and fulfillment in life?

Ask yourself this: what if there is something we can have in our lives that gives us lasting fulfillment and deep happiness that can't be destroyed or taken away from us and that will never fail us or let us down?

Sounds too good to be true, doesn't it? Well, what if I told you that there really is something, anyone can have it, and furthermore, it's free! So what is it? How do I get it? And how do I make the most of it?

Interested?

Then read on . . .

Real fulfillment and lasting happiness that never leave you or fail you can only be found through having God involved in your life and having a friendship with Him. What do I mean by a friendship with God? Well, to understand that fully we have to go right back to the beginning where it all started . . .

In the beginning there was God—and God created people. People represents us all—boy / girl / young / old—so when you read this story you can put your name wherever it refers to people. God created people so that He could share His love with us and so that we could have a friendship with Him. God was pleased with what He had made and thought that people were great. Equally, people thought God was pretty amazing too, and they were best friends. This is how God intended it to be. Everything was perfect, and God and people lived like this for some time—happy in paradise—until one day people did something that changed everything.

Even though God had been nothing but caring and loving toward people, and had provided them with the perfect life and been their best friend ever, they decided they wanted to go their own way and do their own thing. So people turned their backs on God and paradise and went off and did things that God had warned them not to do. People started to do bad things that they knew were wrong, and the result was that, not only did they hurt themselves and others, but most of all, they ruined the perfect friendship they'd enjoyed with God.

It became impossible for people to have the same relationship with God again because the wrong things they had got involved in created a big barrier between them and God. The Bible calls these wrong things *sin*. Sin is everything we've ever said, thought, or done that is wrong and against God's ways and purposes for us. You may be thinking, *Well, I haven't been that bad; it's not like I've killed someone or something.*

But the Bible says that "All have sinned and are not good enough for God's glory" (Romans 3:23). This basically means that all of us have done something wrong whether it was big or small, and God sees it all the same—as sin. Perhaps the biggest thing we have all done wrong is to have ignored God, turned our backs on Him, and said that we don't want Him involved in our lives, even though He is the one who made us! So, all of us were in this position of being on the other side of the barrier—separated from God by our sin.

When God looked at the situation, He was totally bummed, because He knew that this bad stuff would lead people to an awful end. The Bible says, "When people sin, they earn what sin pays— death" (Romans 6:23). So, even though people had made this mess, God had a plan to stop people from destroying themselves and to get rid of that barrier of sin that kept them apart from Him.

His plan was to send Jesus Christ to earth. Though Jesus is called the "Son of God," He was also God Himself in the flesh—God as a human. Jesus was sent to earth to show people a way out of their mess.

No one seriously doubts that Jesus Christ existed—the Bible contains four books about His life and historical research has shown them to be reliable in what they tell us about Jesus. However, the question is, was He who He claimed to be—God in the flesh, God in human form?

Jesus did all sorts of amazing things in His time on earth (you can read about them in the books of the Bible about His life—Matthew, Mark, Luke, and John), including healing people, speaking wise words, and all sorts of miracles. However, Jesus said that His real purpose for being born was to die. Pretty strange thing to say, huh? What Jesus was referring to was the huge significance attached to His death.

You've probably heard the Easter story of when Jesus was executed by being nailed to a huge wooden cross. Well, a lot more was going on than just a good man being executed for making some mad claims. People deserved punishment for the wrong stuff they had done, but instead, Jesus accepted the blame and took the punishment in their place. Jesus was sentenced to death, even though He hadn't done any-thing wrong—ever—and was even found innocent at His trial. So when Jesus died, He paid the price once and for all, for all of people's sin, thus removing the barrier between people and God. This meant that God could forgive people and that the way was now free again for them to have a friendship with God like before—if they want it. God will not force anybody; it is up to each individual. But the opportunity is now there, equally for everyone. It is a free gift that you can choose to accept or reject. "God loved the world so much that he gave his one and only Son so that whoever believes in him may not be lost, but have eternal life" (John 3:16).

Of course the story does not end there. Three days later, Jesus came alive again—something we call The Resurrection. Hundreds of people saw Him alive again and were amazed, even though Jesus had warned them this would happen. The Resurrection proved that Jesus really was who He said He was—no ordinary man could come back to life again. Shortly after this, Jesus told His followers that it was time for Him to go back to be with His Father in heaven. At first Jesus' friends were upset and didn't want Him to go, but then He reassured them by telling them that it was actually better for them if He did go, because He was going to leave behind a helper for them—the Holy Spirit. Jesus explained that if He stayed as He was, He could only be in one place at one time like any human. But if He were to go, He would leave behind the Holy Spirit to help and guide all Christians all over the world at the same time. It is the Holy Spirit, God within us, whom we have with us today, in the new millenium. It is through the Holy Spirit that God guides us, speaks to us, and shows His power to us today.

Christians are not perfect, they're people who've been forgiven!

A Christian is not a super-human who is perfect and has never done anything wrong. You do not have to be perfect to be a Christian. A Christian is an ordinary person like you and me who has admitted that they've done wrong and has asked Jesus to forgive them. They've asked Him to become their friend and to help them live 100 percent for Him. Not only are they forgiven and get to be with Him forever after they die, they also get a better life now with Him helping, guiding, and loving them every moment of every day.

Jesus said, "I came to give life—life in all its fullness" (John 10:10). God has a specific plan and purpose just for you. So what are you waiting for?

And the Prayer . . .

Life to the full through a friendship with God is just one prayer away. You don't need any fancy or special words to pray, but you can use the words below and make them your own if it helps you:

God, I believe that you are there, and I'm sorry that I have spent so much of my life ignoring you.

Thank you that you care about me and want to relate to me as a friend so much that you died for my sins. At the moment it feels like I hardly know you, but I really want to get to know you better.

I know that in the time I've spent ignoring you I've screwed up a lot and done lots of things wrong. I wish they hadn't happened, and I want you to know that I am sorry. **Please forgive me.**

Thank you, Jesus, that you died on the cross for me. I now give control of my life to you. I want to trust you completely with every part of my life and put you first. Holy Spirit, help me to **live my life 100 percent for God** *and give me the strength to know Him more as each day passes.*

Amen.

If you prayed this prayer, or one like it, God has totally forgiven you for everything you've done wrong and accepted you as one of His own children. There is a party going on in heaven right now, celebrating the fact that you have joined the family by becoming a Christian!

Now that you have prayed this prayer, it is a good idea to tell someone you know and trust in the next twenty-four hours.

2 WHaT Do I DO NoW, and WHeRE DO I Go from HeRe?

Though you've probably just made the most important decision of your life—and might I add, the *best* decision of your life—in many ways that was the easy part. Now that you've made a commitment to God and decided to follow Jesus with your life, you may be feeling a little unsure of what you've decided. Let me reassure you that all of these feelings are perfectly normal. Being a Christian is all about having a friendship with God, and I want to give you a few guidelines to help you know where to go from here and also what to expect. Living out your new life with Christ is not always an easy road, but believe me, it's worth it.

The Best of Best Friends

Your new friendship with God is a bit like a marriage. It requires a commitment to the relationship from a motive of love rather than just an agreement or contract. If you got married but then never spoke to your husband or wife, spent time with them, or tried to get to know them better, it wouldn't be much of a marriage, would it? Instead, you would find out what they like, what pleases them and makes them happy, and then you'd spend your time trying to do just that. It is the same with our new friendship with God. If we really want to make a go of it, then we want to find out more about God and how He wants us to live.

Our aim in life, as Christians, is to live a life that is pleasing to Him and to become more and more like Jesus. The Bible says, "You are God's children whom he loves, so try to be like him" (Ephesians 5:1), and "In your lives you must think and act like Christ Jesus" (Philippians 2:5). As I'm sure you can imagine, there are some distinct advantages to having the all-powerful God of the universe on your side as your best friend. Forget "my dad's a policeman," "my dad's the creator of everything" is

> "The night I became a **Christian** was the best **buzz** I have ever had."
> —Claire

slightly cooler, don't you think!? But, joking aside, it is important that we realize that, although God is absolutely huge and more amazing than we can even begin to get our head around, He is also interested in the tiniest details of our everyday lives—what concerns us, concerns Him. He is "King of kings" but also the "friend that sticks closer than a brother" (1 Timothy 6:15, Proverbs 18:24). Basically, God is the best friend we can ever have. We can tell Him absolutely anything and everything, and He is always there for us and never lets us down. He is also a father to us—but not like our earthly fathers who sometimes make mistakes because they are human—God always knows what is best for us. He disciplines us like a father. "God is treating you as children. All children are disciplined by their fathers" (Hebrews 12:7), but He also loves us and wants to look after us: "How much more will your heavenly Father give good things to those who ask him" (Matthew 7:11).

You may have heard Christians describing themselves as being "born again." This is because the Bible describes our asking God into our lives as being re-born. First Peter 2:2 describes us as "newborn babies." We start our lives again in a way—it is a new and fresh beginning when everything bad from our past can be left behind—but we have to learn to live our new life with God: "If anyone belongs to Christ, there begins a new creation. The old things have gone: everything is made new!" (2 Corinthians 5:17); "But you were taught to be made new in your hearts, to become a new person. That new person is made to be like God— made to be truly good and holy" (Ephesians 4:23-24).

A New Life

This means we must be ready to make changes in our lives. But don't worry, this is not something you have to struggle with yourself or get right straight away. The most important thing is that you have made a commitment to God and have asked Him into your life. God will help you to live it for Him by his Holy Spirit, and there is the help

now what

"Changing my old bad ways was one of the most difficult things when I first became a Christian, but I've got some really special Christian friends and they have helped me a lot. I realized that when I made a commitment to God it was about being a Christian 24/7, not just when I felt like it!"

—Abbey

and support of Christian friends. You don't lose your personality when you become a Christian. You won't be expected to wear a tea-length flowery dress, complete with white socks and sandals as soon as you make a commitment. You keep all the good things about your personality—that is how God made you. You are unique and God loves you as you are. The point is that God wants to help you get rid of all the not-so-good things about you and add a whole lot more good stuff in their place!

Ephesians 4:21-24 gives us a helpful formula to adapt to a new way of living that is pleasing to God: "I know that you heard about him, and you are in him, so you were taught the truth that is in Jesus. You

"I realized that you shouldn't **compare** yourself to anyone else and how they are doing. You have to just **listen** to God and to what he **wants for you**, personally, which means learning to **understand** when God is trying to tell you something."

–David

were taught to leave your old self—to stop living the evil way you lived before. That old self becomes worse, because people are fooled by the evil things they want to do. But you were taught to be made new in your hearts, to become a new person. That new person is made to be like God—made to be truly good and holy."

Just trying to do what we think is the right thing won't work—we must make the decision to leave our old way of living first. It would be like trying to fit a brand new set of clothes over lots of layers of old shabby ones—it would be uncomfortable and would restrict your movement. However, if we let Jesus take away the old clothes—all the wrong we've done or are doing—He will then give us just one garment to wear that is new and wonderful and comfortable. (Often in the Bible, Jesus' righteousness is described as gleaming-white linen garments that He gives us to wear: this was considered one of the finest materials around during Bible times.) Once we have changed our clothes, we can then change and be made new in the attitude of our minds and in our hearts, and then start to add the new, good things into our lives.

First of all, there is something to leave behind and put off—our old self, then there is something to change—our attitude of mind and heart—and then something to become or put on—our new self.

Another way of thinking of it is like you're drinking a coke and then you change your mind. You realize milk is a lot better for you, and you want to drink that. You can't just pour the milk in the glass with the coke. You've got to pour out the coke (our wrong and old ways of living), clean out your glass (change of heart to follow Jesus), then start drinking the milk (the things of God—His ways and living for Him).

However, it is important to know that God does not wait for us to be perfect before He loves and accepts us. Romans 5:8 tells us that

"I realize now that I can still have just as much **fun**, or even **more**, being a **Christian**. I can still keep all my **friends** and have as much fun, but now I just have some **guidance** and back-up to help me."

-Abbey

-Abbey

"Christ died for us while we were still sinners"—that means while we were still doing wrong. Some things you may have been doing or ways you may have been living may take a while to change, and that is okay. The main thing is that you have asked Jesus into your life, and as long as you are open to Him and want Him to, He will gradually help you to change at a pace that He knows is right for you. He will highlight things that need change *as* and *when* you are ready. It is important that you understand this and are not forced by others to change at a faster pace than you can cope with. At the same time, you must not avoid things in you that you know need changing. Get someone (an older

Christian friend or youth leader) to help you to work through these issues on an ongoing, regular basis.

You Are Not Alone

If we try to change solely in our own strength, we will not be able to keep it up, but the good news is that we are not alone. As well as help from others, we have a much greater helper, an invisible and powerful friend—the Holy Spirit. After Jesus was raised to life and before He returned to heaven to be with His Father, He promised that He would not leave us alone: "I will ask the Father, and he will give you another Helper to be with you forever—the Spirit of truth . . . he lives with you and he will be in you" (John 14:16-17). The Holy Spirit is not like Casper the Friendly Ghost. He is God coming to live in us to help us and to guide us as soon as we ask Jesus into our lives. We can't see Him, but we know He is there

Remember this formula: something to get **rid of**—old self; something to change—**attitude** of mind and heart; something to put on—**new self**

"One of the things that held me back from becoming a Christian at first was that I wanted to do a good job at being a Christian and I didn't think I could do it. But somebody told me that God does not want you to wait until you are perfect, you can just come as you are. That really helped me and started to boost my confidence."

-Abbey

because we feel Him guiding us. The Holy Spirit is a bit like your new conscience, which helps you to know what is right, what is wrong, and what pleases God. We can ask the Holy Spirit to help us to act in the right way in situations, to help us make important decisions, and to generally help us to live our lives in the right way for God: "But you are not ruled by your sinful selves. You are ruled by the spirit, if that Spirit of God really lives in you" (Romans 8:9); "Live by following the Spirit. Then you will not do what your sinful selves want" (Galatians 5:16).

"Some of my **friends** at school gave me **grief** when I became a **Christian** and that was **really hard**, but all my closest friends were **cool** about it and were **happy** for me."

-Claire

When the Holy Spirit is active in our lives, we start to live our life in a way that is pleasing to God: "But the Spirit produces the fruit of love, joy, peace, patience, kindness, goodness, faithfulness, gentleness, self-control" (Galatians 5:22–23). The Holy Spirit can make a really big difference in our lives. Through Him, God is always with us, so that we are never alone. Our part is to keep in touch with Him and listen to Him, making sure that we do not ignore His presence in our lives: "We get our new life from the Spirit, so we should follow the Spirit" (Galatians 5:25).

Often when people say that God has spoken to them, it is the Holy Spirit giving them a deep "knowing" of something that they didn't know.

what do i do now . . .

Silence is weird" was a famous slogan for a wireless telephone company. Most of us agree that communication is a good thing—after all, we don't get very far without it. You don't get that shirt you wanted for your birthday, to go out with the guy or girl you dig, or that shoulder to cry on without communication. Any kind of relationship needs communication if it is to be a successful one. Your best buds wouldn't be too happy if you never talked to them about what's going on in your life, and sometimes we need to ask for help, to simply share what's on our mind, or share some exciting news. If you are a Christian (or thinking about becoming one), it is basically all about having a friendship with God. This means you need to start talking to Him. This is called *prayer*.

There are many myths about prayer, such as you have to kneel down by the side of your bed with your eyes closed and hands together and use big, long, fancy words—NOT SO! This means you talk to Him just like you'd talk to your best friend, except it's better because you can talk to Him anytime and anywhere about absolutely anything and everything.

Prayer is simply **chatting** to God.

God always hears your prayers, always listens, and always answers them. However, it may not always be in the way you want or expect Him to answer them. Someone once said that God answers prayer in one of three ways:

No—that's not My will for you.

Yes, but not yet—it'll be in My perfect timing.

Yes—go for it now!

So be prepared to accept whatever God's answer might be. But remember, He always knows what's best and always wants what's best for you.

Did you know that prayer . . .

→ doesn't have to be out loud, it can be in your head?
→ doesn't have to be on your own, you can pray with a group of friends?
→ doesn't have to be a list of things you ask for?
→ can be telling God about things going on in your life, or letting Him know how great He is?
→ can be thanking God for how He has helped you?

I can remember a series of significant answers to prayer when I particularly needed to hear from God about my future. I'd finished my final exams in high school and applied to college to do media studies and journalism. However, what I really wanted was to be a singer. But this seemed unrealistic to me and my teachers even advised me against it. I had to agree with them that it seemed more like a dream than an achievable ambition. But, I couldn't get away from the fact that singing was my heart's desire—surely, that was an indication of my life-calling, wasn't it?

now what

I got offers from all the universities I applied to, but then I received a letter saying one of my majors was not available anymore. In the meantime, I had found a more practical major and had thought to myself, *This is my chance not to be stuck doing something I don't really want to do for four years.* So I said to God: "Okay, I don't mind going to college, if I can do this new, more practical course I have found."

So I said to God: "Okay . . ."

I applied, feeling quite confident that I would be accepted, as the required grades were low in comparison to the other schools that had already accepted me. You can imagine how devastated I was when the slip was returned with a big *REJECTED* stamped on it. I couldn't understand it. Why had God allowed me to be accepted for the courses I didn't want to do, which needed high grades, but rejected me from the only one I really wanted that required much lower grades? I was disappointed and confused, so I decided to pray.

At first, I felt nothing, and then a song came into my head. I gradually realized that God was trying to tell me something through a deep "knowing" and peace that I most definitely did not have before. He seemed to be saying, *Trust in Me, because I love you.* I couldn't explain it, but I just knew it was God talking to me. I felt totally different about the whole thing.

At first, nothing changed, but two weeks later it did. There were only a few weeks left before I was supposed to go to college. While I was reading a magazine, an ad leapt out at me. It read, *Are you a Christian and want to learn to sing and dance? Auditions being held for the School of Creative Ministries—Christian Performing Arts School.* I knew this was for me! I went for my first-ever audition and made it!

The next hurdle was the fee—a couple hundred bucks that I didn't have. So again, I prayed about it. Over the next couple of weeks, I miraculously got the money for the first semester through anonymous gifts and donations from friends and family. I decided that I would trust God for the other two semesters. So off I went to London and had an amazing year growing closer to God and receiving training for the arts. As a result of that year, I worked as part of a choir singing with Sting at the Brit

> **"Amen" means "so let it be."**

Awards and then I went on to join the World Wide Message Tribe, which led to my being a part of Shine. By praying, God heard me, guided me, and opened doors for me to reach my heart's desire.

In case you are a little lost for words at times and are not sure what to say to God or where to start, here are a few prayers that you can use, on a few different subjects that you might face. But remember—you do not have to use any special formulas to pray—you can talk to God in your own words any time, and that is more than good enough!

Temptation

Lord, you know everything about me, including my weaknesses. Please give me the strength to overcome all things that pull me away. from you, especially _____, which I am struggling with at the moment. Help me to keep away from situations that make it difficult for me to stay strong. Thank you that you always love me.

If you find praying difficult . . .

→ Try having a **prayer timetable** of different things you want to cover in prayer, e.g. MON . . . Family

> TUES . . . Friends
> WEDS . . . Thank God
> THURS . . . People who need help
> FRI . . . Help to live for God
> SAT . . . World issues
> SUN . . . Church life

→ Try setting a specific time to pray each day (e.g. before you go to bed or before school/work)

→ Try starting a "prayer triplet"–meeting regularly with two other friends to pray together

→ Try going for a walk somewhere quiet and praying

→ Try putting on some Christian music or worship music as you pray

→ Try praying short prayers throughout the day rather than a set long period

now what

Please be with me today and guide me in my thoughts, words, and actions. Amen.

The only temptation that has come to you is that which everyone has. But you can trust God, who will not let you be tempted more than you can stand. But when you are tempted, he will also give you a way to escape so that you will be able to stand it. (1 Corinthians 10:13)

Doubts

Lord, lately I have been having some doubts. I've experienced you in my life, so I know you are there. Please help me to feel you are there. Let me feel you with me every moment of the day. Help me to speak to someone who can help me to find answers to my questions, so that I won't have reason to doubt anymore. Thank you that I know you died on the Cross and that you love me enough to do this for me. Amen.

Then Jesus told him [Thomas, his disciple], 'You believe because you see me. Those who believe without seeing me will be truly happy. (John 20:29)

Friendship/Relationships

Lord, thank you for my friends and all the people you have placed in my life who are important to me. Help me to treat people as you would want me to. Help me to forgive others as you have forgiven me and to put their needs before my own. Help me to be kind to everyone, but give me wisdom to befriend those that will draw me closer to you and to spend less time with those that make it difficult for me to follow you. Amen.

A friend loves you all the time, and a brother helps in time of trouble. (Proverbs 17:17)

Some friends may ruin you, but a real friend will be more loyal than a brother. (Proverbs 18:24)

Putting God First

God, sometimes it is so easy to become swamped by life, and sometimes I allow myself to get too busy and forget to give you the time you deserve. I know that you always have time for me, though, and I want to make you first priority in my life. If there is anything in my life that I hold as more important than you or that distracts me from you, please show it to me and show me how to deal with it. Lord, help me to have you at the center of my life and build everything else around you. Thank you for your promise that if I put you first, then you will take care of everything else. Amen.

The thing you should want most is God's Kingdom and doing what God wants. Then all these other things you need will be given to you. (Matthew 6:33)

Struggling with Living Out the Christian life

Thank you, Jesus, that you loved me enough to die for me. Help me to live my life for you 100 percent. Sometimes I find it so hard to be what you would want me to be every day, but please help me to try my best and to aim to be more like you. Help me not to go back to doing things that I used to do before I knew you. Thank you that life to the full is only found in you—I don't want to miss out on that. Fill me with your Holy Spirit every day to enable me to be what you would want me to be. Amen.

Do not change yourselves to be like the people of this world, but be changed within by a new way of thinking. Then you will be able to decide what God wants for you; you will know what is good and pleasing to him and what is perfect. (Romans 12:2)

Sharing Faith/ Telling Others

Lord, you have made such a difference in my life that I don't want to just keep you to myself. Help me to have boldness and not to miss an opportunity to talk about you with friends and family who don't yet know you personally. Please let the subject come up in a natural way and give me the right words to say and the answers for any questions they may have. Most of all, Lord, may you show in my life by shining through me in everything I do. Amen.

You are a light that gives light to the world . . . you should be a light for other people. Live so that they will see the good things you do and will praise your Father in heaven. (Matthew 5:14-16)

Forgiveness

Lord, lately I have strayed from your path and have gone wrong,

now what

doing things and acting in ways that I know I shouldn't. I'm sorry! Thank you, though, that you died for me on the Cross and forgave me for all my wrongs. Help me to live a life worthy of you, who have now made me a new creation! Help me not to keep making the same mistakes, and help me to accept that you have forgiven me and to move on with my life. Thank you for your grace—the undeserved favor of God. Amen.

Create in me a pure heart, God, and make my spirit right again. Do not send me away from you or take your Holy Spirit away from me. Give me back the joy of your salvation. Keep me strong by giving me a willing spirit. (Psalm 51:10-12)

Future

Thank you, Lord, that my life is in your hands. You know my dreams and heart's desires and that I really want to please you with my life. Please guide my thoughts and help me to make wise choices concerning the future. It seems so scary right now, but I know you

I know, without a doubt, that when you pray things happen. If I could only tell you how much it's changed my life! God hears every prayer and He won't ever let you down—although He might not answer in the way you expect.

-Hanne

have everything in control. Help me not to worry about it but to trust in you. Amen.

Depend on the Lord in whatever you do, and your plans will succeed. (Proverbs 16:3)

So you can see that you don't have to use fancy long words to pray. Just chat to God in your own words. Jesus has some great advice for us on the subject of prayer: "When you pray, you should go into your room and close the door and pray to your Father who cannot be seen. Your Father can see what is done in secret, and he will reward you. And

now what

when you pray, don't be like those people who don't know God. They continue saying things that mean nothing, thinking that God will hear them because of their many words. Don't be like them, because your Father knows the things you need before you ask him" (Matthew 6:6-8).

4

GeTTiNG YouR HeAD AROuND the BIBLE

A Guide Book for Life

Starting to read the Bible can seem very daunting at first and perhaps a little boring because it is so big. However, there are lots of things that can help you.

The Bible is God's Word to us and is very important. It is a bit like a guide book for life, our own manual for living this life the best way— as God wants us to. It has information, instructions, and answers to most things that you come across in life. It really is quite an amazing book — but it is so much more than just a book. Although God Himself did not physically write the Bible, He did inspire all of the authors who wrote its contents. The Bible says that "all Scripture is given by God and is useful for teaching, for showing people what is wrong in their lives, for correcting faults and for teaching how to live right. Using the Scriptures, the person who serves God will be capable, having all that is needed to do every good work" (2 Timothy 3:16–17). The Bible is made up of sixty-six different short books, from history books to poetry books telling about the future. It is split into two main sections — the Old Testament (before Jesus was born) and the New Testament (Jesus' life and after).

> The Gospels are a good place to start as they tell us about Jesus' life.

The Bible is described as "God's Living Word" because it is more than just writing on pages; it is powerful and life-giving: "God's word is alive and working and is sharper than a double-edged sword. It cuts all the way into us, where the soul and the spirit are joined, to the center of our joints and bones. And it judges the thoughts and feelings in our hearts" (Hebrews 4:12).

The Gospels — Matthew, Mark, Luke, and John — are a good place to start. They tell you all about the life of Jesus. You can find them in the New Testament (the second half of the Bible). There are special teen versions of the Bible and also teen study notes, all written in modern language, so they are easier to understand. They're designed to help you get the most out of reading the Bible. I recommend the *Extreme Teen Bible*. Most Christian bookstores will have them, as will many regular bookstores. If they don't, they can order them.

> The first time I ever felt God speaking directly to me was through the **Bible**.

The more we read the Bible, the more we begin to understand God's design for life and how to live it to the full. It helps us to keep on the right track: "How can a young person live a pure life? By obeying Your word"(Psalm 119:9). The Bible is also the main way that God "speaks" to us, by communicating His views and advice on all the things we face, as well as giving us warnings and guidance. It also tells us how much God loves us and what He thinks of us.

God Can Speak to Us Through the Bible

The first time I ever felt God speaking to me was through the Bible. I had not been a Christian for very long — a few months — when I attended a youth event where some teens from the US were over in the UK singing and dancing and performing drama sketches in schools and talking about their faith. The group made such an impact on me that I remember praying, *"God, this is so what I want to do with my life. If I can use my love for singing and dancing and tell others about you at the same time, that would be my dream come true."* I went home that night and prayed to God that one day He would give me my heart's desire. I then opened my Bible, desperate to hear from God. To my amazement, the page it opened on directly spoke to me. It was Ecclesiastes 11:9 and was titled "Advice to Young People." It said, "Young people, enjoy your-selves while you are young; be happy while you are young. Do what-ever your heart desires, whatever you want to do. But remember, God will judge you for everything you do." I was amazed. I couldn't believe how God was so concerned with me and my dreams, enough to tell me to go for it! I held on to that promise from God, and He gave me my heart's desire. Now I am working where I get to enjoy all the things I love: music, singing, and dancing, along with the most important thing in my life — my friendship with God.

That is just one example of when God has spoken to me through the Bible, but there have been many other times when He has used the Bible to guide, warn, or answer me about other things.

Here are some answers to a few of the commonly asked questions concerning the Bible:

→ *What if I don't understand it?*

Before you read the Bible, ask God to help you to understand what you are about to read and how to get the most out of it. Try rewriting what you have read, but write what you think it is saying in your own words. If you are really stuck, ask a Christian friend or youth leader to explain it to you.

→ *How often should I read it?*

There is no set time or amount that you should read the Bible, but the more regularly you read it, the more what you are reading will start to stick in your mind—and the more that happens, the more you will have answers to other people's questions and know what to do in different situations. Furthermore, the more we read the Bible, the more we get to know God and how to live our lives for Him, and the more our faith will grow. So, there are many advantages to getting into a routine of reading the Bible regularly. However, don't set yourself so much to read that you get bored or don't take it in because it's too much to remember. But at the same time, always try to read in sections rather than individual verses. This way, you get the whole picture of what is being said, including the background and setting.

The more we **read** the Bible, the more we get to **know** God.

→ *When should I read the Bible?*

As with finding a suitable prayer time, each case will be individual to each lifestyle. However, a good tip is: Don't read the Bible when you are really tired—you won't be able to concentrate or remember what you've read. So if you know you are not a morning person and don't usually wake up until after first period, perhaps breakfast reading is not the slot for you. Equally, if you love your bed, perhaps last thing at night is not your ideal time. Find a suitable time and place where you won't be disturbed.

→ *What should I read in the Bible?*

The Bible is not like a novel that you would read from front to back, cover to cover. It is made up of lots of separate and very different books. Each one stands on its own, so you can pick any book to start working through. As I mentioned before, the gospels Matthew, Mark, Luke, and John, in the New Testament (the second half of the Bible), are a good place to start; they tell us all about Jesus' life. We can get to know Him better by reading about the things He did and what He was like. If we want to know what God is like, we can look at Jesus; the Bible says, "No one can see God, but Jesus Christ is exactly like him. He ranks higher than anything that has been made" (Colossians 1:15). Jesus also said, "Whoever has seen me has seen the Father" (John 14:9).

Some of the books near the beginning of the Bible, in the Old

Testament, can be a little heavy-going for new Christians. So it might be a good idea to leave them until you have been a Christian for a little while. Having said that, Genesis (the first book of the Bible) is a great book to read to see how it all started! So pick one book to start working through, and perhaps set yourself the goal of reading a chapter a

The Bible is made up of lots of separate and very different books, and each one stands on its own.

day. If you cope with that okay, why not read one of the Psalms each day as well? Psalms are songs and poems written by all sorts of people and cover many subjects, from praise to encouragement to help. They can be very uplifting and are fairly easy reading. You can find the book of Psalms in the Old Testament, towards the middle of the Bible. Try getting into the habit of memorizing bits of the Bible. Start with a short verse or two. Once it is in your memory, it can have more effect in your life.

→ *How do I apply the Bible to my life daily?*

Even though the Bible was written hundreds of years ago, it is called "God's living word" because it is still relevant to our lives today. God's Word will never fade out or go out of date. Admittedly, there are cultural differences, where times have moved on, but the basic principles of living still stand just as strong today. The Bible is full of help, advice, and answers on things like relationships, sex, money, careers, and most other issues that we face today. In all situations, it is important that we know what God thinks on the subject, what He wants us to do, and how He wants us to be. All this is in the Bible. One exercise that may help you apply God's Word to your life is to write out what you have read in the Bible and try applying it to a situation you are in or may face in your life. Write down what you think the verses are saying to you and how they would help you, or what they show you about something you are dealing with in your life. Look at the life of Jesus, or of other characters in the Bible, and see how they reacted in situations or how God helped them.

Remember, **don't worry** if you miss a day; **God** is not holding a **score chart** on you!

n o w   w h a t

The Bible is full of **good advice** and guidance for life. It sometimes has the bad image of being just a book full of a load of **rules** and **regulations** that are there to spoil our fun. However, most of the **lessons** we can learn from **people's experiences** in the Bible and the **teachings of Jesus** are there to protect us and show us how to live life in a way that is not only best for us, but is also **pleasing** to God.

– Tash

Never be afraid to ask an older Christian friend or youth leader for help if you are struggling with the Bible.

5

CHuRCH and YoUTH GRouPS

Many people have a typical picture (stereotype) of what they think church is like and what it is all about. Sometimes those stereotypes can have some truth in them, but often they are just a distorted picture of what it's really about. My earliest memory of church was being dragged to Sunday school when I was about five years old and being bored out of my brain. As you can imagine, I was not too revved to go again.

My next encounter with church was not until I was fourteen. My mom had just become a Christian and asked my sister and me to go to church with her. She wanted to make sure that we didn't just go on what our friends at school had said—or even what she had told us about it—she wanted us to make our own opinion of church and

Christianity for ourselves, from our own experience. We agreed that this was fair enough.
Well, I agreed to go along, expecting it to be
very boring, with creepy church organ music
and filled with old ladies in their hats and
gloves looking down their glasses at me. I
couldn't have been more wrong! Yes, it was strange,
but it was definitely not boring. The church I went to was
filled with people of all ages, including other teenagers, and the music
was provided by a live band, complete with drums and electric guitar!
I was not used to seeing people dancing around and singing to Jesus,
but I could see that these people definitely had something I didn't. My
stereotype of church had been very wrong.

It's **important**
to find a church that
is right and **suitable**
for YOU!

What is Church For?

I'd like to wipe out a few more myths. Going to church is not what
makes you a Christian—you could go to church every Sunday of your

life and it would not make you a Christian. Believing in Jesus and what He's done for you by dying for you is what makes you a Christian. Christians go to church because it is good for them and because they want to, not because they have to. For example, if you are a U2 fan, it is not a chore to go one of their concerts—you want to go, no one has to force you. In the same way, church is a great place to learn more about God, grow closer to Him, and to spend time with other Christians.

Church is not a building; it's when **Christians** get together.

Church is not a building, as many may think; church is a gathering of Christians. So you can have "church" by meeting together with other Christian friends during the week, not just on Sunday.

There are many different types of Christian churches, because there are many different types of Christian people. Some like to worship God in a quiet, meditative way, while others like to worship in a loud singing, dancing way. No church is better or more right in God's eyes. The question is, *Which church is right and suitable for YOU?*

"Now that I am a **Christian,** I don't think that church is **boring** anymore. I used to think it was just full of old people, with a choir. It is more fun than I thought it would be."

—Claire

Church can be a bit of a culture shock at first, so try to go with people you know. If it's a church that loves Jesus and teaches the Bible, has people of your age, and if you stick it out, you will definitely get lots out of it. You may be surprised and find that you enjoy it!

Youth Groups

It is very important that you begin to spend time with other Christians that you can talk to and who can help you. It's also fun meeting other Christians your own age, as you can help each other.

The person who gave you this book should be able to put you in touch with a good church youth group in your area. There will be people who would love to get to know you and help you in your new

> "Because **none** of my **old friends** are Christians, I know it would really help me to make Christian **friends** with people I feel I can be **myself** with as a **new** Christian."
>
> —Claire

friendship with God, or anything else you may need. One of the things that was most helpful to me when I first became a Christian was the church youth group. I attended it from age fourteen until I was eighteen years old. Not only did I have lots of fun, but I also made some life-long friends and got a great foundation of knowledge about Jesus and the Bible at a pace I could handle.

It is also a good idea to attend a new Christians' group or course, if there is one being taught. This way you don't feel that you are the only one just starting out, and you can be with other people who are asking the same questions. It is also encouraging to learn with others, and progress and grow together.

now what

"My Christian friends have really **helped** me. They are totally **normal** people, and most of them have been through the same problems as me, so that's useful. I **trust** them and I can ask them stuff and know that their advice is sound! Even if I feel like I'm asking them a **stupid question**, I don't feel **embarrassed**. Some of them are my role models."

-Abbey

Someone To Look Up To

No matter how determined you are to make it, there will be times when you will find it tough to be a Christian and will need some extra help. That's why it is a good idea to develop a friendship with someone you can be accountable to. This person should be someone you know and trust, and who has been a Christian longer than you have. A youth leader is a great choice for this role, for all of the above reasons, but it doesn't have to be. Make sure you are regularly in touch with this person: ask any questions you have and talk about any problems that may come

"My youth group was what helped me the most when I first became a Christian. The youth leader spent a lot of time teaching us from the Bible and helping us to understand some very complex issues. He answered all the questions I had. My youth group was a place where I felt that I could make mistakes and learn in a safe environment. I know that without the help and support that I constantly received, and am still receiving, from my leaders and friends, I would not be here now as a Christian. Church, and especially the youth group, helped me so much to have a greater understanding of Jesus and who He is."

-Lucy

up. Talking is a great help, but having someone like this praying with you and for you is even better. Don't be worried about asking someone if she/he can fulfill this role (disciple you)—any older Christian will feel very privileged to be asked, and will enjoy helping you to get the most out of your new life with God.

now what

"Having an older Christian to talk to and ask my questions to has helped me. I needed to have what Jesus had done on the Cross explained to me, and needed to be able to ask my questions privately without feeling they were stupid. In the beginning, I didn't know how to pray and felt like I needed to be perfect straight away. By talking and asking questions I have begun to understand what it's really all about and what is important."

-Claire

6 TeLLiNG OTHeRS—SHaRiNG YouR FaITh

Once you begin to settle into your new life with God, you should start to share it with other people that don't know Him. Like any good news, you will want to share Him with the world. For example, if you had the cure to cancer it would not be fair—neither would you want—to keep it to yourself. Likewise, the brilliant news about Jesus and what He has done is for everybody, and in a way, we have a responsibility to share that with as many people as we come into contact with. Telling others about Jesus is called "evangelism." So why is this so important, and why should we tell others about Jesus?

Why Should We Tell Others About Jesus?

Jesus commanded us to. In Matthew 28:19 Jesus tells His disciples

(His followers—so that means you, too) to "go and make followers of all people in the world. Baptize them in the name of the Father and the Son and the Holy Spirit." So we should evangelize out of obedience to Jesus, because He tells us to. But we should also do so out of a desire to see others experiencing the great life that we enjoy with Jesus at the center. The other reason is to ensure that others have the chance to accept Christ, be saved from hell, and receive eternal life through Him. Evangelizing may seem a bit scary to you at the moment, but don't worry. For starters, it is not something you have to do in a forced and unnatural way. If Jesus is central and the most important thing in your life, then He will shine through you anyway. When Jesus is in your life, He will affect all areas of it and others will see that in your speech, behavior, and in your way of handling situations. There are many ways that are far more effective than standing on the dining tables at lunch time and preaching to your whole school, so breathe a sigh of relief. Often, the best way to share Jesus with your friends is to show them rather than to tell them. This means letting them see Jesus in your life, by the way you act in different situations and the things you join in or don't join in. This gives a clearer message than merely forcing your opinions on others in a judgmental way. All that would do is earn you the nickname "Bible-basher." It is important not to behave towards your friends as though you think you are better than they are.

How Should We Tell Others About Jesus?

There are many ways to tell others about Jesus, and there will certainly be one that suits you and will come so naturally to you that you won't even realize you are doing it! As for *how* to do this—there is no set way, but here is some basic advice which might help you:

Be yourself! Don't act in a way or use words you wouldn't normally, either to try to impress or to fit in with the people you are talking to. Just share what Jesus has done in your life in a natural way. The biggest tool for evangelism you have is your life story (your testimony). How and why you came to know Jesus is totally personal to you and no one can argue with that, add to it, or take away from it. Tell them a little bit about what you were like before you became a Christian, how and why you came to know Jesus, and then something of what your life has been like since. Make sure you are confident in it; practice it and aim to keep it around three minutes (not longer).

Be natural! Try not to work or force Jesus into every conversation you have with people in an unnatural way. Don't make people projects to convert, but seek to be a friend first and foremost; this way you will be more effective and people are more likely to listen when the subject does come up. Again, if Jesus is central to your life, the subject will come up naturally, especially when those around you see the amazing change and good things that God is doing in your life. At the same time, don't be ashamed of your faith or try to hide the fact that you are a Christian. Jesus was not embarrassed about you when He died on the Cross for you. So make sure that you are bold about sharing Him with other people—you never know, you may be a part of changing their life forever!

Be honest! Be prepared to tell people what the difference is in your life when they ask. Don't miss an opportunity through panic or embarrassment to share what Jesus has done in your life. Equally, if you do not know the answer to a question someone asks you, just be honest and say so. You can then offer to find out for them, from an older Christian or youth leader who may know.

Be bold but not arrogant! You may be worried about being picked on or made fun of for saying you're a Christian. But remember, a bully will bully just about anyone. When others see that you are not embarrassed about it, they will begin to respect you for your beliefs. If they don't, then they are too immature and should be ignored. Before I was a Christian, I was known for having a big mouth and being vocal about my opinions, so when I became a Christian I was pretty much the same, except I talked about Jesus instead and was always ready to answer any questions that any one would ask me.

Some Advice from the Bible on Evangelism

Pray that I can speak in a way that will make it clear, as I should. Be wise in the way you act with people who are not believers, making the most of every opportunity. When you talk, you should always be kind and pleasant so you will be able to answer everyone in the way you should (Colossians 4:4-6).

Stereotypes of church and Christianity can put people off. This is because, unfortunately, somewhere along the way there has been some truth in those stereotypes. However, a true and clear picture of Jesus Christ generally does the opposite. You only have to take a look in the Bible to see how amazing Jesus was and is, and how people were drawn to Him. So our job is to make sure we are good imitators of Him and show a good picture. Let's represent Him well!

"Telling others about Jesus can either be the **cringiest** or the **easiest** thing that you can ever do. If your faith is truly part of you then nothing needs to be forced. **Be confident!** You've found something amazing, and the less embarrassed you are, the more other people will wonder what it is that you've got!"

-Nic

now what

7 QUeSTIoNS, DouBTS, and FeARS

This chapter covers the most common questions, doubts, and fears that new Christians have. The whole point of this book is to help you to get the best start you possibly can in your new life with God. That means you must feel free to have doubts and ask questions, too. It is not wrong to have questions. In fact they can help you to grow in your faith, as you learn more when you find out the answers.

Common Questions, Doubts, and Fears

Do I have to follow loads of rules and are there things I can't do as a Christian?

Christianity isn't just a list of dos and don'ts; although there are guidelines that are there to help us, because God knows what is best

"A friend explained to me that in the Bible Jesus' **disciples** were actually looking at him after he was raised from the dead but they still **doubted**. When I heard that, it helped me to accept that it was **okay** to have **doubts** and that there were going to be some **questions** that I just wouldn't have the answers to."

-David

for us. There is a Bible verse that says: "'We are allowed to do all things,' but all things are not good for us to do. 'We are allowed to do all things,' but not all things help others grow stronger. Do not look out only for yourselves. Look out for the good of others also" (1 Corinthians 10:23-24). This means that God gives us the freedom we want, but He wants us to use that freedom wisely. Also, it is worth noting that the so-called "rules" are often misquoted, and so people miss the point as they take them out of context. At first, it can be difficult to understand why God says that things like getting drunk, and having sex outside of marriage are not a good idea, especially if this has been "normal" for us before we

now what

experienced God. However, with a bit of thought we can work out why God advises us on most things—it's because He knows what's best for us and wants us to experience that to the full.

What if I can't give up my old ways right away?
It would be too much for us, and God doesn't expect us to completely change everything at once, especially if we want lasting results. As soon as you ask Jesus into your life, you receive the Holy Spirit (see Chapter 2). "Whoever confesses that Jesus is the Son of God has God living inside, and that person lives in God" (1 John 4:15). The Holy Spirit himself will change you in many ways—and possibly quite quickly—within your first year of you being a Christian.

When we receive Jesus we begin to understand what is good for us and what isn't, and we want to work at adapting our life to please Him. So if we have been doing specific things that we know are not good, such as smoking, stealing, and fighting, it is usually not too difficult to deal with these things fairly early on in our life as a Christian.

However, it is more difficult to change things like our attitudes and ways of thinking, because human beings are creatures of habit. A good place to start is realizing that being a Christian means giving God complete control over your life. He is not just an extra on top of the rest of your life; He should be the center of everything. It takes a while to maintain a consistent and steady relationship with Jesus, and sometimes you may feel like it's just not happening at all. It is common to have an initial period when you seem to sail through, followed by times of being up and down and having many doubts and questions—this is normal!

The main thing is to realize that it is not your behavior that determines whether you are a Christian or not, it is your heart. God looks at the heart and loves us all the time, whether we seem to be doing well or not. So it doesn't matter if you don't get everything sorted out right away. Walk through all issues with an older Christian you trust,

God changes our hearts, but we have to work on changing our minds to catch up with that.

and pray and ask God for help—He will deal with everything in you in His perfect timing, as and when He knows you are ready for it. The most important thing is that you want to and are aiming to be like Jesus: "God began doing a work in you, and I am sure he will continue it until it is finished when Jesus Christ comes again" (Philippians 1:6).

What if I do something wrong again?

Let me tell you now, you will definitely do something wrong again; otherwise you would be perfect—and Jesus was the only person to have walked this earth who was perfect. Your aim should be to live a life that is pleasing to God, but you will make mistakes because you are only human. Forgiveness is not the issue here—Jesus has already forgiven you for all your wrong when He died for you on the Cross. It is important that we believe this—either the Cross has said it all, or the Cross has said nothing at all. "I write to you, dear children, because your sins are forgiven through Christ" (1 John 2:12). Jesus died once and for all. He didn't just *cover* your sins; He took them away completely.

The word the Bible uses for this is "atonement." If we believe in Jesus and why He came, and have asked Him into our lives, we receive the benefit of His forgiveness: "God loved the world so much that He gave his one and only Son so that whoever believes in him may not be lost, but have eternal life. God did not send his Son into the world to judge the world guilty, but to save the world through him. People who believe in God's Son are not judged guilty. Those who do not believe have already been judged guilty, because they have not believed in God's one and only Son" (John 3:16-18).

Jesus was the **only** person to have walked this earth who was **perfect.**

So then, what should you do when you go wrong? First, tell God that you are sorry and then ask Him to help you not to make the same mistake again. Don't dwell on the fact that you have messed up—God doesn't. Deal with the problem, put it right if possible, and then move on. If it is a problem that keeps happening, find someone you trust to talk through it and help you with it.

Will I have to stop hanging around my old friends?

No. God certainly does not want you to abandon your friends when you become a Christian. In fact, He wants you to keep in touch with them so that you have opportunities to tell them about Him. You can often be a great example to people who knew you before you were a Christian, because they will see the most change in you. However, it is important that you are a good example for your friends and not a bad one. They will be watching your life to see if God really does make a difference. It is therefore important that you do not join in with things that you know are not going to please God or be good for you. If your friends are true friends, you should find that they will respect you for this, although, at first, it may be hard for them and you if these are things you used to do together regularly. Why not try introducing your old friends to your new Christian friends and perhaps invite them along to youth group?

There may be some people, though, who it may not be helpful for you to keep hanging around with. If someone consistently makes it too difficult for you to live out your new life with God, and if they keep pulling you back into your old ways, it may mean you need to spend less time with them. Our friends have a huge impact on our lives, and we should always choose them carefully. "Do not change yourselves to be like the people of this world, but be changed within by a new way of thinking. Then you will be able to decide what God wants for you; you will know what is good and pleasing to him and what is perfect" (Romans 12:2).

What if my family are not Christians?

Sometimes, if your family are not Christians, it can be difficult for them to cope with the change in you. This is because they have known you all your life and know you very well—yet you have made a big decision that may not have had anything to do with them. They may think it is just a phase you are going through or that you've just gone a bit weird for a while (a member of my family thought I'd been brainwashed!). However, it is important that you are a good example to your parents or guardians by honoring them and doing what they say. The mother of one of my friends actually banned her from going to church and youth group at one point and refused to let her be baptized. Instead of disobeying her, she respected her mom, even though it was difficult— she had to wait about six months and then her mom finally agreed. Once they begin to see the amazing difference God makes in you, your family will gradually begin to see that you are serious about the decision you have made and may even start showing an interest themselves.

Can I have a girlfriend/ boyfriend who is not a Christian?

There is nothing to stop you from having a friendship with someone who is not a Christian, but having a boyfriend/ girlfriend who is not a Christian is not a good idea. The main reason for this is that such relationships hardly ever work without you having to compromise your beliefs at some point. As a Christian, you are going in a different direction than someone who is not a Christian. Picture it this way: Having a relationship with a non-Christian is a little bit like you standing on a chair, and them standing on the floor. If you have ever tried this you will know that it is much easier to be pulled down from the chair than it is to pull the other person up onto the chair with you. As a Christian, I went out with someone who was not a Christian once, and it

> It is much **easier** to be pulled **down** than it is to pull the other person **up**.

was one of the most stressful periods of my life. It was horrible not being able to share the most important thing in my life with my boyfriend. In the end, I realized that I couldn't please both parties, and I had to choose between my boyfriend and God. This decision can determine the whole course of your life and is not an easy one to make when your emotions are involved. The Bible says this on the subject: "You are not the same as those who do not believe. So do not join yourselves to them. Good and bad do not belong together. Light and darkness cannot share together. How can Christ and Belial, the devil, have any agreement? What can a believer have together with a non-believer?" (2 Corinthians 6:14-15).

What if I get picked on or lose friends because I've become a Christian?

Not everyone will understand why you have become a Christian and this may bring some difficulties for you. People these days are not used to others having strong and definite beliefs, and they can feel threatened by someone who has different beliefs than them. However, a bully will bully someone for any reason at all—whether you are wearing the right shoes or have a trendy enough haircut. Being a Christian is just something else they can pick on. Bullies are weak people who pick on someone different, just to make them feel bigger and better. Although this can be tough to face, their opinions are worth nothing. If you are convinced of what you believe and are not embarrassed about it, they will soon get bored of picking on you. As for friends, if they do not respect your beliefs and the decision you have made, are they worth having as friends in the first place? I found with many of my friends that once they knew I was a Christian they thought it was cool that you could be a Christian and still have fun and laugh, even though they could see I was trying to do the right things. They would also end up coming to me to talk if they had any problems and would even ask me to pray about things for them!

Do I have to go to church every Sunday?

You do not have to go to church every single Sunday, but I hope, as you get to know God better, you will want to go as often as you can. Church is not supposed to be a boring chore that you attend out of obligation; it is meant to be a place where you can go and enjoy learning more about Jesus and worship God, while meeting with other Christians. There are things you'll like and not like about church, as with most things, but it is all good for your growth as a Christian. It is a bit like the food we eat—it is easy to eat chips and ice-cream and other yummy stuff, but when it comes to sprouts and liver (yuck!), that's a different matter. However, a balanced diet is essential if we are to be healthy. To make it easier for you, make sure that the church you go to loves Jesus and teaches the Bible and has a good youth group with people your own age.

> *If God is there, then why do bad things happen?*
Most of us have wondered about this question at some point or other—and if you haven't, then you may well be asked it by one of your friends—as it is something many people don't understand. Sometimes, when we look at the world or turn on the TV and watch the news, we can wonder where God is in the midst of the mess. There is so much crime, violence, and hatred in the world today. It is easy for us to point the finger at God and blame Him. However, God hates all the bad stuff that goes on, and His heart breaks for us when He sees us suffering. The thing is, God made us with the fantastic gift of "free will." This means we have the freedom to choose to be as bad as we want or as good as we want. Unfortunately, a lot of the bad in the world is a result of human beings choosing to do wrong. Sometimes people even cause suffering and say it is in the name of

Jesus, when of course it has nothing to do with Him.

When it comes to sickness and natural disasters, it is difficult to find an answer that comforts us. But we have to remember that things in the world got messed up when mankind first decided to rebel against God and started to sin (do wrong). In the beginning, the world was perfect—it had none of these problems—just as God intended it to be. When mankind went his own way, things got turned upside down. This is why there are unexplainable things happening all the time. Although it can seem unfair that God allows these things to happen, we know that He does not cause them. However, one day He will return and put everything right!

We have the **freedom** to choose to be as **bad** as we want or as **good** as we want.

If God made us, who made God?

This is a hard question to get your head around, but no one actually made God. God has always been there and always will be. God is the creator and we are the created. If something or someone had created God, then He wouldn't be God—they would. Everything starts and finishes with God. He is outside of time and all-powerful, so nobody made Him.

How do you know that God is real?

Although we cannot see God, it does not mean that He does not exist. There are lots of things that we can't see that we know are real. For example, we can't see electricity, but we know that it's there because we can see the effects of it when we turn on an electrical appliance. It is the same with God: Although we cannot see Him we can see and feel the effects of Him being in our lives. Our experience of Him shows us that He is there and real. Furthermore, I think we only have to look around at the wonderful things in the world to see signs of God everywhere. Sometimes it may feel as if God is not there or that He is not listening to what you are saying, but just because you can't always "feel" Him there, does not mean He isn't there. At times like this, try to remember how you felt when you first became a Christian and what made you want to make that decision.

If God is good, then why does he send people to hell?
The whole issue of heaven and hell really comes down to the decisions we make while we are alive here on Earth. God does not force us to do anything—we have free will. Jesus actually spoke more about heaven than he did about hell. The reason God sent Jesus was to give everyone the opportunity to accept Him and to find their way to heaven through Him. However, if someone goes through their whole life here saying, "God, I don't want to know you, I don't want you to have anything to do with my life," then God will remember the decision they have made when their life ends. Heaven is basically eternity with God, which means everything good, and will be more wonderful than we can begin to imagine. Hell is eternity without God—the reality of this will actually be a lot worse than we can imagine.

*What if I have doubts about the
decision I've made to be a Christian?*

As I have said all along in this book, it is okay to have doubts and
questions—and you will have them. The question is what to do with
them when they do come up. It is important not to keep them to yourself. If you do, they will build up until you have steam coming out of
your ears, and you'll want to give up. Instead . . .

→ *Find someone to talk to.*

They may not be able to answer all your questions, but they can certainly try, and it helps so much to get it all out in the open. The chances
are that they have had the same doubts and questions themselves at
some point in their lives. This will help you to realize that you are not
the only one.

→ *Be honest.*

Be truthful about how you feel, even if you feel bad for feeling that
way. It's okay to be totally honest about what's going on in your
head—it is the first step to being closer to an answer.

→ *Ask God.*

God knows everything—He knows how you are feeling and wants to help you find a satisfying answer. Sometimes there won't be an answer for us to understand because God's ways are often different from ours, and we will never understand everything while we are here on earth. But God can give us peace so that we no longer worry about it anyway.

→ *Don't worry.*

Having doubts and questions is all part of growing up as a Christian. It is a good sign that we want to know why we believe what we believe. Not only does this help us to answer other people's questions in the future, but it also gives us a good base for a lasting faith through good times and bad times.

"God has given me a joy inside so that, no matter what bad things happen to me, I know God is with me and will get me through the situation, if I just turn to Him and ask for help. I don't feel lost anymore. For a long time I felt lost and didn't have a purpose, and now I've got that purpose—to please God."

-David

"Most people have questions and doubts about their faith, especially when they are first getting to know God. The only time that this is a problem is when the doubts are not talked about. God is not threatened or intimidated by our doubts and questions. Asking questions and confronting doubts make your faith deeper and more secure in the end."

-Nic

TeN FiRST STePS for the NeW CHRiSTIaN

1. *Make sure you are a Christian.* Have you prayed the prayer?

2. *Tell someone.*

3. *Set a regular time to spend with God.* Get alone with God and read the Bible.

4. *Pray.* See Chapter 3.

5. *Make Christian friends.*

6. *Find a church and youth group that you like.*

7. *Find an accountability friend,* a Christian you look up to.

8. *Get baptized.* This is only for when you feel ready. Baptism is when you get submerged (dunked) under water or sprinkled on the head with water (different denominations do it different ways). It sym-

bolizes leaving your old life behind as you come up from the water. It is a declaration of your faith and a display of commitment to God.

9. Memorize God's words.

10. Ask for help when you're struggling.

In conclusion, I just want to encourage you to go for it and not look back: "As you have received Christ Jesus the Lord, so continue to live in him. Keep your roots deep in him and have your lives built on him. Be strong in the faith just as you were taught, and always be thankful" (Colossians 2:6-7). You can make a whole world of difference! And I have some great advice for you, especially for young people, straight from God's Word: "Do not let anyone treat you as unimportant because you are young. Instead, be an example to the believers with your words, your actions, your love, your faith, and your pure life" (1 Timothy 4:12).

GO FOR IT!

Don't be **lukewarm**. If you are, you will have such a **miserable** life. The most **boring** people I know are luke-warm Christians—neither hot nor cold. Love God with all your heart—that's what He wants; He wants your **heart**. I promise you, life is **exciting** when you live it **HOT** for God!"

-Hanne

CHeCK iT OuT!
GeT INVoLVeD!
MaKe a DiFFeReNCe!

www.j2000usa.org
Find out what's going on in Africa. Love your neighbors in this global village we live in.

www.adiccp.org
You can help the kids of the Chernobyl nuclear disaster live longer. Find out how.

www.volunteermatch.com
Enter your zip code and find out how